Ride Like the Wind

A TALE OF THE PONY EXPRESS

by Bernie Fuchs

THE BLUE SKY PRESS

AN IMPRINT OF SCHOLASTIC INC. • NEW YORK

FOR MY DAUGHTER, CINDY

B. F.

THE BLUE SKY PRESS

Copyright © 2004 by Bernie Fuchs
All rights reserved.

SCHOLASTIC, THE BLUE SKY PRESS, *and associated logos are*
trademarks and/or registered trademarks of Scholastic Inc.
Library of Congress catalog card number: 2003009636
ISBN 0-439-26645-9
10 9 8 7 6 5 4 3 2 1   04 05 06 07 08
Printed in Singapore   46
First printing, March 2004
Designed by Kathleen Westray

"AWAY ACROSS THE ENDLESS DEAD LEVEL OF THE PRAIRIE A BLACK SPECK APPEARS AGAINST THE SKY, AND IT IS PLAIN THAT IT MOVES. WELL, I SHOULD THINK SO! IN A SECOND OR TWO IT BECOMES A HORSE AND RIDER, RISING AND FALLING, RISING AND FALLING—SWEEPING TOWARD US NEARER AND NEARER—GROWING MORE AND MORE DISTINCT, MORE AND MORE SHARPLY DEFINED—NEARER AND STILL NEARER, AND THE FLUTTER OF THE HOOFS COMES FAINTLY TO THE EAR— ANOTHER INSTANT A WHOOP AND A HURRAH FROM OUR UPPER DECK, A WAVE OF THE RIDER'S HAND, BUT NO REPLY, AND MAN AND HORSE BURST PAST OUR EXCITED FACES AND GO SWINGING AWAY LIKE A BELATED FRAGMENT OF A STORM."

—MARK TWAIN
NEVADA, 1861

As Twain traveled by stagecoach, the driver alerted
passengers that a Pony Express rider was coming.

Storyteller's Note

THE STORY IN THIS BOOK TAKES PLACE in Nevada in 1860, a time of dramatic changes in our country. Despite their strength and courage, a small band of the Paiute tribe, led by Chief Numaga, had barely survived a treacherous winter. Frontiersmen, moving westward, had killed off herds of bison and had cut down forests of precious nut trees. How would the Paiute live without them?

Now the Pony Express Company was building stations, fifteen to twenty miles apart, across Paiute land. Young riders carried mail from station to station, racing as fast as they could. The stations were another intrusion. Against the pleas of Chief Numaga, Paiute warriors attacked and burned some of the stations in a futile attempt to hold back the inevitable.

Yet on the settlers came—men, women, and children heading westward—and with them, orphan boys like Johnny Free, who also showed enormous courage and have their own stories to tell.

*T*WO HOURS BEFORE dawn, the sound of galloping hooves startled Johnny Free into action. In minutes, a rider would bring the mailbag to Camp Creek Station, and Johnny's leg of the Pony Express would begin.

Johnny pulled on his boots and tied a holster to his thigh. Then he went outside. As soon as the rider arrived, Johnny quickly flipped the special mailbag from the rider's saddle to his own. Then Johnny and his beloved pony, JennySoo, bolted out of the station at full gallop.

It was a bright, blue, moonlit night. Johnny wondered if the wolves were watching from the bluff above the clearing. He felt a kinship with the ever-present, curious wolves. Like Johnny and the native Paiute people, they were survivors in this unforgiving Nevada land.

Suddenly, Johnny's Paiute friend, Little Grey Fox, was beside him. Little Grey's pony, Pinyon, was the only horse around who was almost as fast as JennySoo. For a few miles, they raced, with JennySoo winning by just a hair. Then Little Grey rode off, saying good-bye with the Paiute peace sign he'd taught to Johnny Free.

Halfway into the journey to Rock Springs Station, Johnny could see a yellow-orange glow on the horizon. As he sped onward in the amber haze of dawn, a black column of smoke rose, dead ahead, in the direction of the station.

The station had been burned to the ground. Johnny knelt and picked up a blackened tin cup. He knew the men must have gone on to defend the next station. But where was the fresh pony he needed to relieve JennySoo?

JennySoo nuzzled his hand. Wiping away tears, Johnny knew he had to keep going with the mail. He swung himself back into the saddle, and they rode like the wind, off in the direction of Rattlesnake Station.

It was a long ride—too long. Exhausted, Johnny followed the trail to a creek that dipped south, and then he stopped to share some biscuits with JennySoo. He stripped her of the saddle, then stripped off his own shirt. He walked her into the creek bed up to her flanks, shivering all the way, then filled his hat with water and doused her head, neck, and back. The coolness perked them both up.

If need be, Johnny thought, JennySoo can still outrun the Paiute ponies. But what about the mail? Johnny dressed, slipped the saddle back on, and hoisted himself up. Leaving the cool creek bed, they headed west under the hot noon sun.

As they rode, Johnny looked around and behind. Even JennySoo kept her ears pricked up and nervously pranced from side to side.

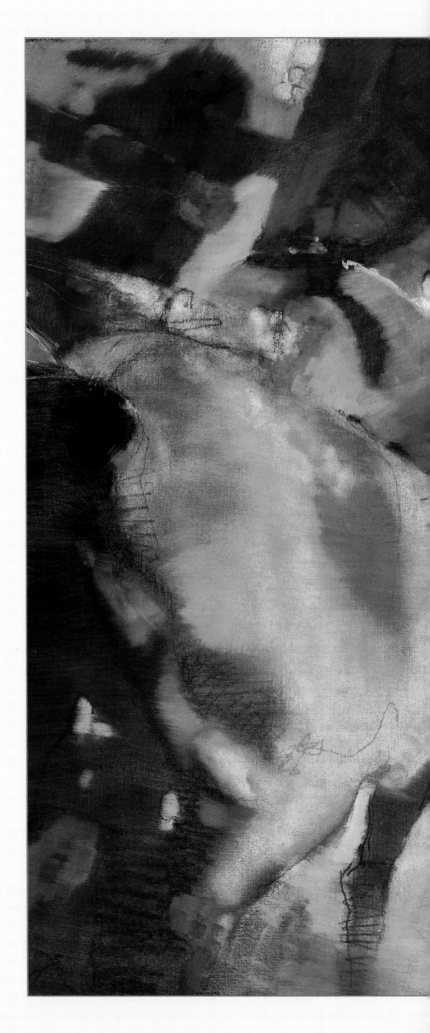

Suddenly, Johnny felt them. Where or how many, he couldn't tell, but the presence of the Paiute was frighteningly real.

With a puff of dust behind a boulder, seven Paiute warriors appeared as if by magic. With a slap of the reins to JennySoo's flank, the race was on.

Arrows whistled past them. Sighting a ridge ahead, Johnny turned sharply toward it, hoping to widen his lead.

Reaching the top of the ridge, Johnny was suddenly jolted out of the saddle as if hit by a thunderbolt. He tumbled down the ridge and quickly scrambled under a ledge. Unsnapping his holster, he drew his revolver. "Run, JennySoo! Run!" he shouted.

The horse took off, and for many miles, the Paiute did not discover she was riderless. She ran and ran, outdistancing her pursuers, and one by one, the Paiute gave up the chase.

Turning back, they gathered just above the ledge where Johnny lay hiding. Cautiously, he unsheathed his knife and clenched it in his teeth. A white-hot pain shot up his right shoulder. Surely this would be a showdown.

To his surprise, the sound of the ponies' hooves slowly receded back over the ridge, leaving him in deadly silence. The pain in his shoulder had turned numb, and blood was running into his hand. He realized he had been hit.

He yanked a piece of arrow out of his shoulder and slowly drifted into unconsciousness.

JennySoo continued on, riderless. She lost no time, and with no weight on her back, she ran even faster along the trail, the empty stirrups banging against her sides.

When she finally reached Rattlesnake Station, men came running. For a moment they cheered to see the pony, but when they saw that Johnny was missing, they fell silent. They tried to hold JennySoo as they took off the mailbag and her saddle, but she reared up, knowing she needed to be free. Johnny was in danger. She turned and ran back on the trail. She must go find him.

The run back to the rocks exhausted JennySoo. Where was Johnny? Surely he was in among the rocks, but she couldn't find him. She circled the rocks again. Nothing.

Suddenly, there he was. All she could do was nuzzle, nibble, and push the boy, trying to bring him to life.

Finally, he opened his eyes and reached up to rub her nose and forehead. "Good old JennySoo," he said. He wondered how long he had been lying there, for the sun was lowering and turning orange.

Johnny began to get up, but the sharp pain in his shoulder stopped him. Pulling on JennySoo's mane, he was finally able to stand and step up onto a boulder.

Still holding onto her, Johnny slid his leg over JennySoo and pulled himself up.

Slowly, with his good arm wrapped around her neck and his cheek pressed against her, they moved along as smoothly as they could so JennySoo would not lose him again.

They made their way onto the trail, back toward
Rattlesnake Station, where they would find help.

They were halfway there when JennySoo suddenly stepped sideways, off the trail. Johnny looked up, and on the ridge, three Paiute sat on their ponies.

Two warriors began to descend in pursuit of Johnny, but the third, Chief Numaga, raised his hand. At this, the two stopped. Without a word from Numaga, they understood that Johnny Free and his pony were not their enemies.

Then, from farther down the ridge, Johnny heard
the familiar whinny of Pinyon, Little Grey's pony.

Johnny knew they were safe and wouldn't have
to run anymore that day.

Johnny Free's shoulder healed, and one morning after racing Little Grey Fox, his friend gave him a gift. It was a beautiful hand-carved wolf that Little Grey had carved out of a branch of a pinyon tree. The Paiute were moving their village, and it would be the last time Johnny would ever see his friend.

Not long after, the Pony Express ended. With the construction of telegraph cables, news could be sent from coast to coast in minutes. All in all, the Pony Express had lasted only nineteen months.

Johnny Free and JennySoo left Nevada and went farther west, to California, to make a life at ranching. JennySoo gave birth to a beautiful brown-and-white colt that Johnny named Little Pinyon, and it's fair to say that he and JennySoo were happy with their lives. But they always remembered their adventures on the Pony Express, and even as he grew to be an old man, Johnny told many tales about it—especially the day that JennySoo returned to find him and save his life.

About the Pony Express

THE PONY EXPRESS WAS ESTABLISHED ON APRIL 3, 1860, to provide the fastest mail delivery between St. Joseph, Missouri, and Sacramento, California. With a trail length of nearly 2,000 miles, the Pony Express had more than 150 stations and employed approximately 183 riders during its operation of just under 19 months. The majority of riders were around 20 years old; the youngest was 11, and the oldest was in his mid-40s. A California newspaper advertisement read: "Wanted. Young, skinny, wiry fellows not over 18. Must be expert riders. Willing to risk death daily. Orphans preferred. Wages $25 a week."

Most riders are said to have ridden 75 to 100 miles per trip and changed horses every 10 to 15 miles; stations were located every 5 to 20 miles. The riders passed mail from one to another along a route that ran through what is now known as Missouri, Kansas, Nebraska, Colorado, Wyoming, Utah, Nevada, and California. The time covered from St. Joseph to Sacramento was approximately 10 days.

The story in this book is a work of fiction, based on a wealth of Pony Express stories recorded in the late 1800s. Although the station names and the names Johnny Free and Little Grey Fox were created by the author, Chief Numaga was a real person and an advocate of peace. Confrontations between the Paiute people and Pony Express riders are known to have happened. It has been said that the Paiute tribe, 6,000 of whom lived in Nevada and Utah, posed a particular threat to the Pony Express, largely because of their poverty, which is said to have led to violence. Their situation in Nevada in 1860 is briefly described in the Storyteller's Note in this book. The Pony Express was forced to cancel service in May 1860, for the first and only time, because of Paiute raids.

We hope *Ride Like the Wind* will encourage young readers to want to learn more about the Pony Express, the Paiute and other Native American people, and the events that took place during this fascinating period in history.